TAPEJARA

NOTHOSAURUS

TSINTAOSAURUS

CAUDIPTERYX

PACHYCEPHALOSAURUS

NEOVENATOR

KENTROSAURUS

OURANOSAURUS

ANTARCTOSAURUS

CHASMOSAURUS

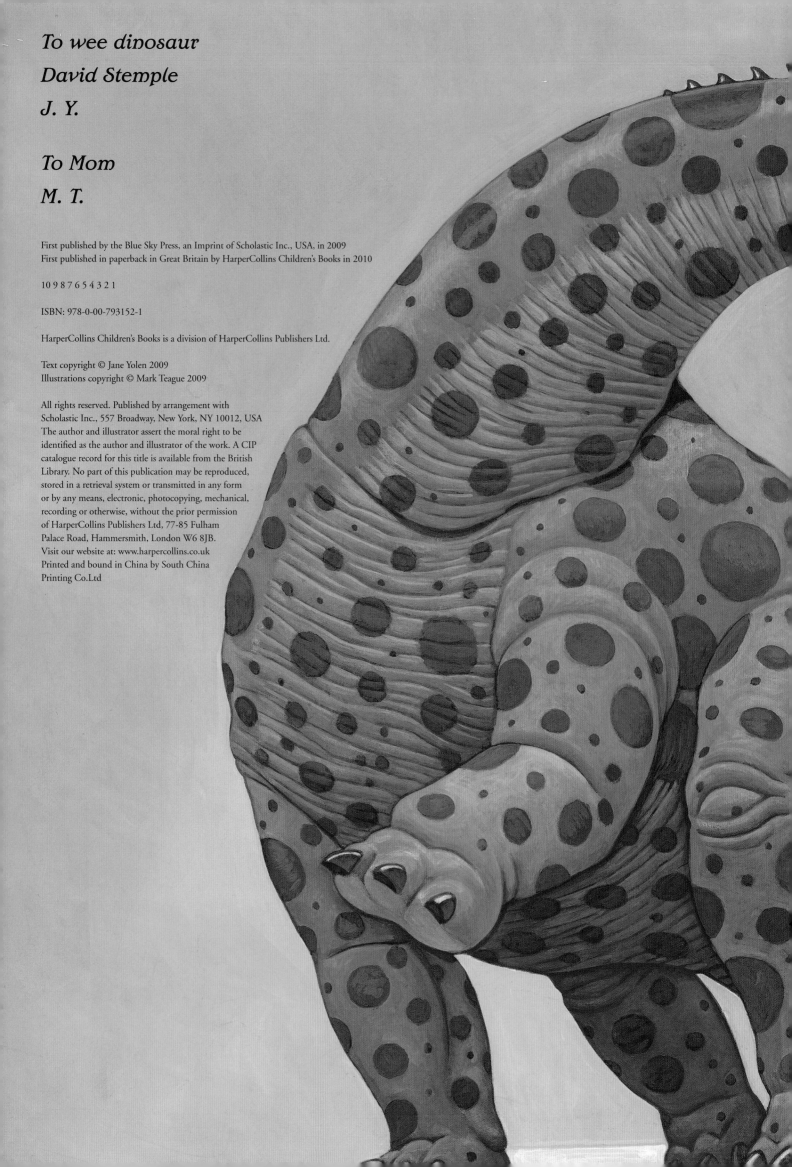

To wee dinosaur
David Stemple
J. Y.

To Mom
M. T.

First published by the Blue Sky Press, an Imprint of Scholastic Inc., USA, in 2009
First published in paperback in Great Britain by HarperCollins Children's Books in 2010

10 9 8 7 6 5 4 3 2 1

ISBN: 978-0-00-793152-1

HarperCollins Children's Books is a division of HarperCollins Publishers Ltd.

Text copyright © Jane Yolen 2009
Illustrations copyright © Mark Teague 2009

How Do Dinosaurs Say I Love You?

JANE YOLEN

Illustrated by
MARK TEAGUE

HarperCollins *Children's Books*

You woke in the morning
in such a bad mood…

then sat at the table
and fussed with
your food.

But then you blew kisses
and waved from the door.
I love you, I love you,
my dinosaur.

Out in the sandpit
you threw lots of sand.

CHASMOSAURUS

You ran from the slide,
after slapping
my hand.

But you suddenly turned
with a smile I adore.
Oh, I'll always
love you,
my dinosaur.

KENTROSAURUS

You moped through your nap time
and slept not a wink.

You flooded the house when you played in the sink.

TSINTAOSAURUS

But you got out the mop
and then cleaned
up the floor!
I love you
so much,
little dinosaur.

Off in the car,
you kept kicking
my seat...

and when we got out,
you were dragging
your feet.

But you held my hand tight
when we walked in the store.
I'll love you forever,
my dinosaur.

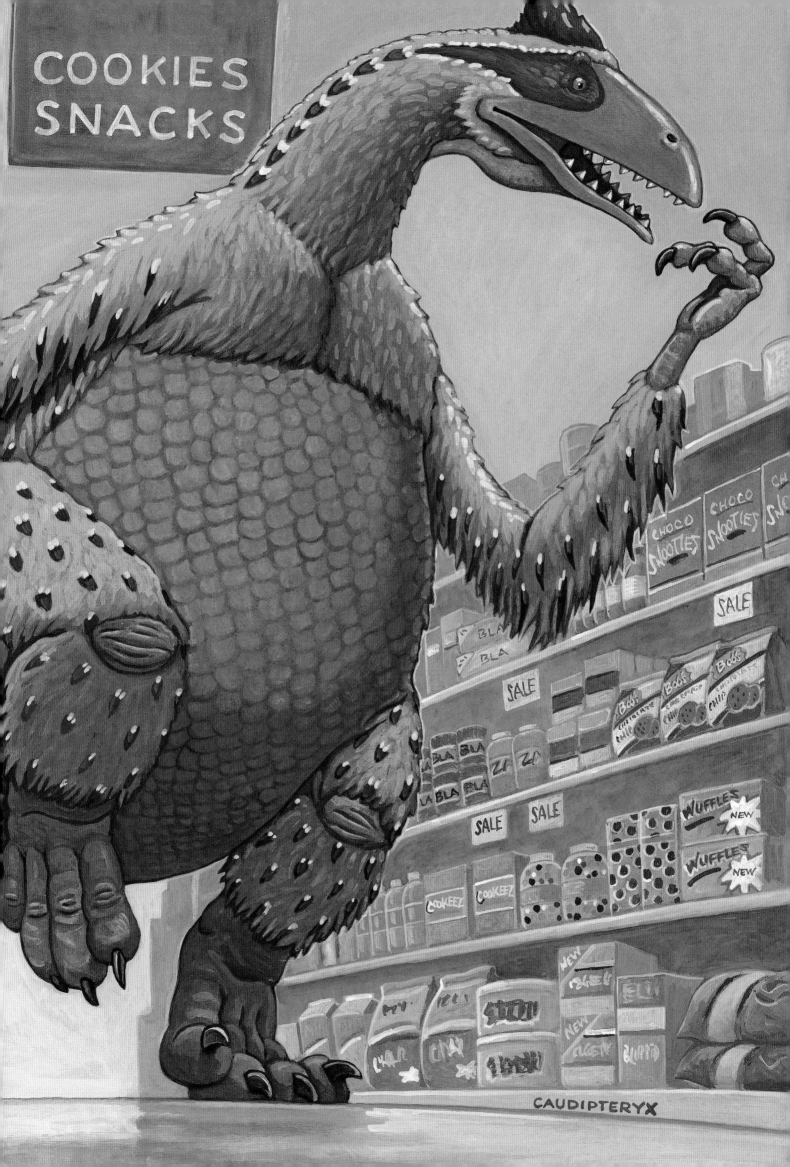

Dinner disaster!

You made such a mess!

Would you stay up past bedtime?

The answer was

YES!

But when you smile sweetly
and hold back your roar,
when you kiss me and hug me
once, twice, even more…

...that's when you give love,
and I know this is true,
because *that's* how a dinosaur says
I Love You!